MEET MEECHE THE MELODIOUS OWL

Written by Mechelle Davis
Illustrated by Brandon C

Xulon Press
2301 Lucien Way #415
Maitland, FL 32751
407.339.4217
www.xulonpress.com

Paperback ISBN-13: 978-1-6628-1695-6
Hard Cover ISBN-13: 978-1-6628-1696-3
Ebook ISBN-13: 978-1-6628-1697-0

Meeche, the Melodious Owl, woke up bright and early with the sun at 6 o'clock to take a shower. She sang, "Whooo, whoo, whooooo! Whooo, whoo, whooooo!" When Meeche finished, she exhaled, "Whooooo, that was fantastic!"

At 7 o'clock, Meeche was brushing her beak. She
made sure to brush every part. While brushing
she hummed, "Mm mmm mmm mmm! Mm
mmm mmm!" She delightedly whispered, "Mmm,
that was wonderful!"

At 8 o'clock it was time to eat breakfast. While Meeche was cooking her oatmeal, she cheerfully sang, "Oh oh ohhhh, oh oh oh ooooooh!" Meeche shook her beak, and exclaimed, "Oooh, the oatmeal sure smells amazing! And it looks delicious!"

At 9 o'clock, Meeche began her daily house cleaning. She happily tweeted, "Me me me me meeeee, la la la laaaaa, ho ho ho ho hooooo!"

While singing and hooting around, Meeche dusted the bookshelves, cleaned the windows, washed clothes, mopped the floor, and vacuumed the carpet.

At 12 o'clock, it was time for lunch, but Meeche's throat felt awfully scratchy, and painful. She worriedly thought, "Maybe I should drink some warm tea, and see if that will help me feel better."

At 2 o'clock, Meeche the Melodious Owl tried her best to sing. All that she could muster up was a sad, "Cough, cough! La laaaa... Mee mee, cough! Ohhh, cough, ohhhh!" Meeche's throat hurt terribly.

Poor Meeche. Poor, poor Meeche didn't feel so great at all. So, she called Dr. Hoot. Meeche tried to tell him what was wrong, but she could hardly hoot a word!

Soon, there was a knock at the door. It was Dr. Hoot! He asked Meeche to tell him about her problem. Instead of Meeche answering, she pointed to her throat. "Oh, I see," sighed Dr. Hoot. "For once, you can't sing a note!" He pulled two plump, bright yellow lemons from his medical bag, and told Meeche, "Take two of these and call me in the morning."

At 5 o'clock in the evening, Meeche the Melodious Owl made a big cup of lemon tea and hurried off to bed. Meeche tossed from one side of the bed to the other. She was restless. Wishfully, she pondered, "I hope I can sing a few notes in the morning."

At 7 o'clock Meeche was still awake, and tears began to roll from her eyes, down her cheeks. Meeche felt so sad and fearful. To help her get some rest, she played some soft music. Soothed by the melody, Meeche fell fast asleep.

The next morning at 6 o'clock, Meeche carefully rolled out of the bed, and gently opened her mouth. First, she sang in a very quiet tone, worried that her throat might hurt again.

By 7 o'clock Meeche realized that her throat felt wonderful, and began to sing out loud with joy! "Me me me me me me meeeee! La la la la laaaaa, ho ho ho ho hooooo!" Meeche was one happy, melodious owl!

The End

Parents, Teachers, and Guardians,

You are the foundation that plants the seed for reading to grow in your child. Research tells us that reading to children every day builds their language and literacy skills. While children actively listen to books, they become engaged in conversations through their prior knowledge and experiences, and develop strong oral language skills. Reading books opens the gates for exploring different reading materials like magazines, cookbooks, take-out menus, and the list goes on! So, take a look, in a book, and get positively hooked!

FUN ACTIVITIES
WITH MEECHE THE MELODIOUS OWL

• Make Meeche the Melodious Owl Clock

• Discuss Meeche's activities at each time of the day

• Move the hand on the clock for each time that Meeche is active.

• Identify the words highlighted in red to learn from
Meeche's Word Bank.

• **Play "What Time is the Clock?"**

• Each time you move the hand of the clock,
have your child say the time, followed by a fun movement!
(Jumping jacks, twist your hips, march in place, etc.)

Check out the website for fun videos on
how to do these activities at home!
HTTP://MEECHESREADERSCLUB.COM

Meeche's Word Bank

melodious
bright
fantastic
delightedly
wonderful
cheerfully
amazing
delicious
happily
awfully
worriedly
instead
pondered
gently
tone

High Frequency Words for Kindergarten - 2nd grade

-a	-me
-all	-of
-and	-one
-around	-out
-at	-see
-big	-she
-but	-sleep
-by	-some
-call	-take
-can	-that
-could	-there
-every	-two
-for	-up
-from	-was
-her	-when

CPSIA information can be obtained
at www.ICGtesting.com
Printed in the USA
BVHW020225020921
615894BV00021B/226